The Adventures of Grover in Outer Space

BY SARAH R...
ILLUSTRATED BY NE...

Featuring Jim Henson's Sesame Street Muppets

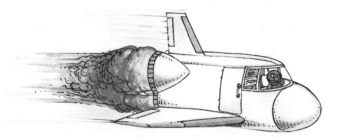

Random House/Children's Television Workshop

"Four, three, two, one, blast off!"

Grover was watching a rocket blast off on TV. It was so exciting!

Grover's mother came in. "It's past your bedtime, Grover dear!"

Grover got into bed and his mother tucked him in.

"Mommy, can I be an astronaut when I grow up?"

"Maybe," said his mother. "But first you need your rest. Good night, Grover."

Grover closed his eyes and thought about what it would be like to be an astronaut.

"Earth to Grover, Earth to Grover," squawked a voice from the two-way radio.

Grover spun around in his special rocket-chair and leaned over the radio.

"It is I, Grover, speaking," he said. "Mission under way. I, Grover, will keep Earth up to date. Over and out!"

Grover looked out of the spaceship window. He could see Earth in the distance. It was a friendly-looking blue and green globe that got smaller and smaller as Grover's ship carried him farther and farther away.

"Bye-bye, Earth!" Grover called. "Bye-bye, Sesame Street!

"Gee," he sighed. "I miss my friends already—and my space trip has just begun!"

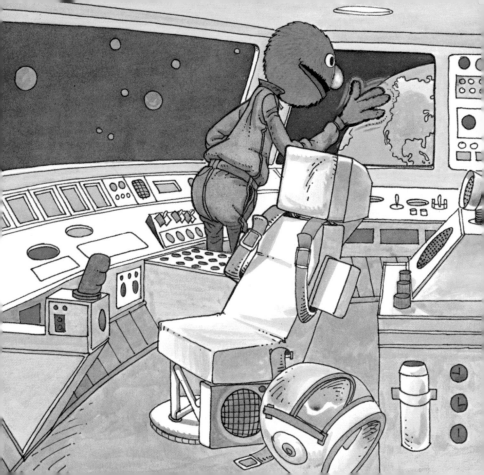

The rocket ship sped farther out into space, past Mars, Jupiter, Saturn, Uranus, Neptune, and Pluto.

"I wonder if there are any friendly monsters living on those planets," Grover said.

Then he saw another planet in the distance.

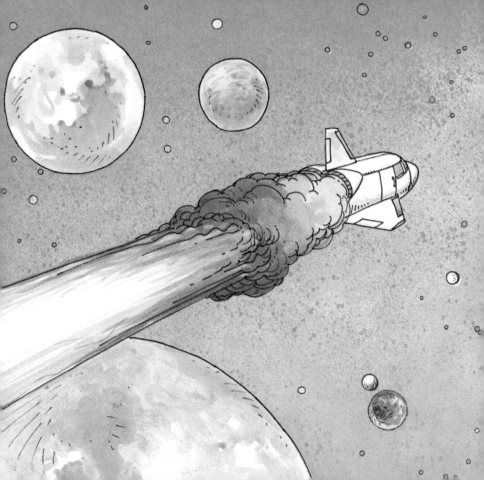

"Which planet can this be?" Grover wondered as his spaceship drew closer. "Have I, Grover, discovered a new planet? I will name it the Planet Grover!"

Grover was so excited, he forgot to steer the rocket carefully. When he looked out the window again, he saw that his ship was heading straight for the new planet.

"Oh, dear! I, Grover, am about to crash-land on my very own planet!"

Grover tried to steer the rocket. He was really very good at steering, because he practiced on his tricycle almost every day.

"Oh, my goodness!" Grover shouted as he landed the spaceship safely on the unknown planet.

Grover opened the door and climbed outside. He was ready to explore. He looked around in every direction and gasped.

"Oh, what is this?" he exclaimed. "The trees on this planet have blue leaves instead of green ones! Blue is my favorite color."

All of a sudden Grover heard a strange sound.

"Meep, meep!"

"I, Grover, do not like strange sounds," Grover said nervously. "In fact, I do not like strange planets— even if the trees do have blue leaves!"

"Meep?"

"I want my MOMMEEEEEEEE!" cried Grover.

Then a small monster poked its head around the spaceship and looked straight at Grover.

"Meep!" said the monster. "My name is Meep. Who are you? And what are you doing here?"

"I am lovable old astronaut Grover and I have come to explore your planet," said Grover.

"I am on my way to school," said Meep. "Do you want to come along?"

"That sounds like fun!" said Grover.

Meep introduced Grover to his teacher and his friends.

Grover looked around the classroom. Everything was blue! The chalk was blue, the clay was blue, all the crayons were blue. There were even blue goldfish.

"What a wonderful planet," thought Grover. "Maybe I will like it here after all."

When it was snack time, everybody sat down to eat.

"Oh, joy!" said Grover. "Even the food is blue!" Grover tried a meep cookie. "Mmm. This tastes as good as an Earth cookie," Grover told his new friends.

Thinking of cookies made him think of Cookie Monster. And thinking of Cookie Monster made Grover think of home.

"I have been away from home a long time," said Grover. "I should get back to Earth soon.

"Meep, I want you to meet *my* friends. Can you come home with me to Sesame Street?"

Meep looked at his blue watch. "I don't think so," he said to Grover. "Mommy Meep is expecting me home for dinner."

Grover hugged his new friend good-bye. Then he climbed aboard his spaceship and blasted off for Earth.

"I cannot wait to tell everyone on Sesame Street about my new friend Meep and the blue trees and the blue cookies."

Grover was so excited about everything he had seen on the new planet that he didn't notice that he was getting closer and closer to Earth. Suddenly the spaceship landed with a great bump.

Grover rubbed his knee and then rubbed his eyes.

His mother came in and picked him up off the floor. "What a bump you had!" she said. "How did you fall out of bed, Grover dear?"

Grover said, "I was not in bed! I was in a spaceship. I was on the Planet Grover and everything was blue!"

"That must have been quite an adventure," said Grover's mother as she tucked Grover back into bed.

"Oh, it was!" agreed Grover. "But now I am glad to be back home. Good night, Mommy."